PEOPLE OF THE TITANIC

30 TALES OF EXTRA-DOOMED SOULS WHO SAILED ON THE SHIP OF DREAMS

SHAWN CARLOW

First Printing: 2025

ISBN 978-1-954158-36-8

Humorist Books is an imprint of *Weekly Humorist*, owned and operated by Humorist Media LLC.

Weekly Humorist is a weekly humor publication, subscribe online at weeklyhumorist.com

99 Wall Street #2012 • New York, NY 10005

weeklyhumorist.com - humoristbooks.com - humoristmedia.com

Cover design and illustrations by Marty Dundics

Book editor: Brian Boone

Author photo by Erick Feigin

PRAISE FOR "PEOPLE OF THE TITANIC"

"Throw some of your allegiance to historical facts overboard and enjoy these funny and imaginative tales of the doomed ship's lesser-known guests."

—**Martha Kelly** (*Euphoria, Baskets*)

"If you've ever wondered what would happen if The *Canterbury Tales* hooked up with *Our Town* and had an illegitimate child on a cruise, then this book's for you."

—**Gregory Martin** (*Jimmy Kimmel Live!*)

"The humorous spin on the *Titanic* we've all been waiting for. Finally a book that bridges the gap between history nerds and comedy nerds."

—**Brian Kiley** (*Conan, The Astounding Misadventures of Rory Collins*)

"I've often thought to myself, 'Why can't accounts of the tragic sinking of the *Titanic* be a bit more... upbeat? Well, my prayers have been answered by this fun-filled romp through the aquatic graveyard! What could be better?"

—**Mark Ganek** (*Archer, The Tick*)

For Yuki.

PREFACE

There are only a few things we can be assured of in life. Ben Franklin's "death and taxes" statement elegantly offers two of them.

But there is another thing that Ben could not possibly have been aware of at the time, as it was more than a century before this thing would exist. It's the *Titanic*. Try to find someone who's unaware of the *Titanic*; go on, I dare you. I bet there are a couple of people out there somewhere, maybe in Wyoming, but let's pretend for the sake of my point here that there are none.

My experience with the ship encompassed the movies: the old black-and-white one with Barbara Stanwyck, and the 1997 James Cameron juggernaut. I read a lot about it over the years, thoroughly fascinated by it. The ship had it all — all classes and kinds of people — and it represented the hopes and dreams of so many of them.

But, in a very personal sense, it began for me as a quiet, awkward child of 11 trying to fit into a larger world, attending science school in Woods Hole on Cape Cod in the summer of 1980. My uncle, Dick Campbell, ran the tiny boatyard there and soon after my arrival, he took me to the other side of the pond that housed the boatyard, to the oceanside, where large, sea-going ships were tied up, part of the Woods Hole Oceanographic Institute's roster of research vessels. He marched me up to one of the boats and immediately began conversing with a man onboard, and behind the man sat a large white submersible atop the boat. Introductions were made and I shook hands with Dr. Robert Ballard, the man who would first explore the *Titanic* with two other people aboard that very same submersible (the *Alvin*) just six years later.

Later, when I was in my teens, I heard a remarkable story from my family, about how my great-grandfather (my mother's dad's father) had almost sailed onboard the *Titanic* but had missed it. Wait, what?! Yeah, it turns out my great-grandfather was back in Scotland visiting relatives, and he rushed to get back but missed the legendary boat, likely sparing his life. If he had sailed, he probably would have been in third class, increasing the certainty of his demise. It would not have affected my grandfather's birth, though, as he was about six years old and living in New Hampshire, but my grandfather may possibly have had a bit more of a touch of melancholy in life, perhaps, having grown up without a dad.

Then while doing standup, I had a joke about a traffic school one block away from us in Encino that existed and was inexplicably named the Titanic Traffic School, and I wondered why anyone would name a driving school after the world's most famous driving accident.

And it wasn't the only *Titanic* joke I had. I had this fictional one, too:

"I saw a documentary about the heroes of the *Titanic* last night. Surely, you know the heroes of the *Titanic*: the captain who stayed at the helm of the ship; the Unsinkable Molly Brown; the band that kept playing as the ship went down. Well, this documentary was about the lesser-known heroes of the *Titanic* — like the Detmer Brothers. They ran a hot dog stand on the top deck, and as the ship was in its final throes, and people were sliding by, they were handing them hot dogs saying, 'Tell all your friends.' And there was also the mime that kept performing as the ship went down, and as the ship turned on its side, he attempted doing that 'invisible rope trick,' all to no avail, naturally.

And now *that* has been elongated into a fictional book. And not everyone in the story is a hero. And you can read the book right now. Please read it.

INTRODUCTION

Let's talk about the RMS *Titanic*, that gleaming ocean liner that was the White Star Line's crown jewel of its day, a testament to both human progress and hubris, that sailed from Southampton on its maiden voyage on April 10, 1912, and sank on April 15 in the chilly waters of the North Atlantic. Heard of it?

Yes, somehow, over 110 years later, the mighty ship still captures our undivided attention, seeming to never leave our side, the bulkheads of our minds pierced by its habitual presence.

But, more importantly, let's talk about the many souls that peopled the vessel and reflected its inner spirit.

Surely, you've heard of some of the people of the *Titanic* – Captain Edward Smith, who reportedly stayed at the helm of the doomed ship as it sank; the "Unsinkable Molly Brown," Margaret Brown, whose spirited entreaties to get the lifeboat she was in to turn around to pick up passengers nonetheless went unheeded; or Wallace Hartley, the man whose steadfast and inspiring musical octet kept playing as the ship went down.

Only 706 people survived the voyage, while over 1,500 passengers met a watery grave, and each had a story to tell. Some were merely minor bit players of meager provision, and some were vibrant, dynamic leaders of state or captains of industry who left a much wider wake with their passing. But they were all important and created the fabric for the tableau that was to unfold there out on that icy sea on that fateful night.

1

The people of the Titanic *numbered 2,240 in total, with about 30 different nationalities.*

And there were certainly some unique people on board.

(1) The Detmer brothers, Andreas and Stefan, were German businessmen staying in second class who ran a hot dog stand on the First Class promenade deck of *Titanic* – the only sanctioned food stand on the entire vessel. If you were in first class, most of the grand ship's food was eaten in the sumptuous café, saloon, or restaurant. A slightly less accommodating but still extravagant eating space awaited those in second; trash chutes served the third-class passengers, delivering the contents of wiped-off plates and leftover soup straight down to the lower decks, where the rabble waited eagerly with their open mouths and collection buckets.

The Detmer brothers peddling their wares.

The Detmer brothers were well known for their antics when preparing frankfurters, catching them in hot dog buns behind their backs or through their legs. Many a hungry passenger marveled at the magical dexterity with which they performed, while also fervently hoping that their meal would not be dropped upon the deck, which most times it was not. Tom Cruise was said to have studied old newsreels of the brothers when he was preparing for his role in *Cocktail*.

The brothers have also been credited with inventing the tip jar — and placing money in it at the start of the day to make it seem like people were leaving money, even if they weren't, because remember, it was mostly wealthy people up on the promenade deck.

The night of the sinking, the stand had been closed for several hours when the ship struck ice, but when their dark fate seemed certain, Stefan Detmer suggested to his brother that they serve warm hot dogs as comfort food to the worried passengers. And a few survivors later told of how, when the ship was in its final throes and tilting downward, the brothers were seen handing hot dogs to people sliding by and entreating them to "tell all your friends." The futility in that gesture was obvious, but, still, you have to admire their gumption.

The two brothers' bodies were never found after the sinking, but remnants of the hot dog stand washed up on a beach in Greenland and were used to make a memorial to the brothers that still stands in Germany. In Hamburg.

---

(2) Jonny O'Neill was an Irish immigrant from Galway who had moved to America eight years prior, following the Parsnips Famine of 1904. Once a year, he would return to the country of his birth to teach Irish step dancing to underprivileged orphans and to carouse around town, which then would lead to a whole new round of underprivileged orphans being born.

Jonny seemed to be born right into Irish step dancing itself, as it was said that when he emerged from the womb, his arms were stuck to the sides of his body at first by his mother's congealed birth juices, but that his legs kicked fast and free. This, of course, led to bruising on his mother's nether regions, but also a standing ovation from the Irish doctor and nurses gathered round.

As he grew, so did the legend of Jonny O'Neill. No one else had the speed and the intricate footwork that he had, and several ruined their feet, permanently, trying to keep up.

On the great ship, *Titanic*, Jonny sailed in second class, but he often made trips down to steerage to impress the immigrants with his dancing skills and to impregnate women.

In the end, no one really knows how many micro-fetuses ended up perishing in the Atlantic that night, but O'Neill is credited with keeping the people in third class calm when all hope was gone and the lifeboats were away, by organizing a spirited jig contest to those that were left behind — and to the winner was promised, "a mouthful of seawater, sure as ye please."

Tens of thousands of his descendants gather every year to mark the occasion of his "disappearance" into the ocean, and the papers thereafter in Galway referred to Jonny as "Jonah O'Neill," because they liked to imagine he was swallowed by a whale after the boat went under and that he still travels from place to place out in the Atlantic Ocean to this day, kicking and dancing inside that whale as it swims along. Of course, that's just lyrical Irish storytelling; he definitely drowned.

---

(3) Sally Newcross, a well-known American political activist, was just 22 when she sailed on board the *Titanic*. She came from a family of individuals who sought to uplift the human race by protesting injustice, but Sally was particularly drawn toward animal protest after an ill-fated trip at age four to a butterfly garden in New Jersey. No one knows why anyone would schedule a butterfly garden for demolition with explosives, but life was different then, and Sally stayed inside the garden enclosure for 15 days with her parents to make sure that nothing would get blown up.

Two years before *Titanic*, in 1910, she had famously chained herself to a postbox in London's Trafalgar Square along with seven other women in support of the animal suffragette movement just then beginning to take hold. The very next year she chained herself to a tree in Times Square to support rabbits' right-to-work laws and then chained herself to a hitching post later that year in St. Louis in support of moths.

Sally was headed back to America on the *Titanic* after picking up pamphlets and more chains at a wholesaler in London, planning to chain herself to the fence outside the White House upon her return, to protest President Taft's shifting views on pregnant marsupials.

While on board the ship, she picked up from one of the galleys an empty crate that had once held milk bottles and overturned it on F deck, near where the animals traveling on the ship were kept and used it as a speaker's platform. It was there that she gave her daily speech, "Sally's Special Animal Report, So Listen Up, *Titanic*."

Sadly, she never made it to Taft's White House at all. Her life ended at a fateful impromptu protest on board the *Titanic*, when she yelled loudly about shark rights and then chained herself to the top of the *Titanic*'s central staircase just minutes before the doomed ship struck the iceberg, and the jarring the ship underwent when it struck was enough to cause her to drop her key off the staircase and into a grate below.

Seventy-four years later, after the *Titanic* was discovered, Sally Newcross was found still chained to the staircase, her notes for President Taft still in a watertight bag found clutched in her hand, and the 27th President never even found out the poor woman's views on marsupials.

2

The Titanic, *that mighty Leviathan, was constructed in the shipbuilding docks of Belfast, Northern Ireland, but its official embarkation point was Southampton in England. It then made stops in Cherbourg, France and Cobh, on the south coast of Ireland, before heading out onto the open ocean.*

And the ship made that first voyage with a whole host of its designers and suppliers onboard, most of whom eventually went down with the ship on which they steadfastly worked.

(4) One such passenger was **Paul Wexton**, the ship's chief bulkhead designer. Wexton was an assistant to Thomas Andrews, the principal shipbuilder, and he sent Andrews all his notes on his bulkhead specifics through Andrews' office via a series of pneumatic tubes. None of the notes ever reached their destination, however, as Andrews' office did not have the pneumatic tube system — the old, leftover one from the company that occupied the office before had long since been disused. Two weeks into his employ, Wexton finally discovered this, finding that his notes were just popping out into an empty field two hundred yards from the office.

Wexton was born on the east coast of England, in Hornsea, on April 5, 1878, and while still in his teens, could be found building metal chambers in his yard that he used to imprison his three, and possibly, at one time, four, sisters. Fortunately, he turned his hobby into the exact job you'd want to have if you wanted to continue building metal chambers, but people get tired of you imprisoning their family, and he started as an apprentice bulkhead designer at the firm of Walleye and Cross. In 1908, he moved on to the White Star Shipping Line, ready to tackle even bigger challenges.

Wexton's watertight bulkhead designs were much sought after in the shipbuilding community, and he would regularly draw all the cool crowds at White Star Line business and social functions. He had become a much-fêted shipping design celebrity, and no one else could show off his own sleek and chic bulkhead portfolio with the flair of Wexton.

Wexton sailed out on that first *Titanic* trip extremely confident in his bulkheads, often boasting about their impermeability, although he fared rather poorly after the ship hit the fated iceberg that night and began to take on water. Thereafter, his boss, Thomas Andrews, also present on that maiden voyage, was spotted honorably helping women and children into boats before losing his own life and was much celebrated in the weeks and years after the sinking. The same cannot be said of Wexton, who came completely unglued, and was seen running naked on all the decks, throwing deck chairs into the sea. His last words were reported to be in the form of a song he invented called "Loveless Bulkheads, Why Won't You Adore Me?" — or perhaps these words he may have shouted down to the water midway through the sinking: "I am the swimming star, Delouis Prenacter, and I wish you to make way for me, sea creatures" — depending on who you asked. But all agreed he was entirely naked, and it was bitterly cold, so...

---

(5) Warren Straithclyde built the bronze cherub that stood at the foot of the grand staircase on *Titanic*'s A deck. Originally, the ship was to have no cherubs at all, as Captain Smith was not overly fond of them, but then some of the other higher-ups pointed out that not having a cherub on your ship was "like not having sunshine or perfumed air."

Straithclyde and his bronze-works just outside of London were commissioned into producing the finished cherub that ended up bringing much joy and happiness to both ascending and descending passengers alike. A habit was even quickly started on the maiden voyage where the people would rub the cherub's nose for luck, but obviously that didn't really work out well for most.

Straithclyde was invited to sail on the initial voyage as a

thanks for his fine, detailed craftsmanship, and as he stood on the prow of the ship, proudly eating raisins and low-cost caviar on toast, the ship set sail.

During the voyage, Straithclyde would often draw up a chair opposite the A deck staircase and admire his handiwork in a sort of egotistical reverie. He thought it might be his finest work yet and would not be denied the pleasure of seeing it in its adopted home.

It was on one such evening four nights in, when the ship gave a sharp bump, as he drank sherry in his cabin, that Straithclyde became aware that something had changed. He walked with purpose to the cherub and stared at it for no one knows how long, until a young man came by and handed him a life jacket. Straithclyde, now awakened to the full nature of the emergency, was last seen taking his life jacket off and placing it onto the cherub.

Straithclyde's body was never found, but the cherub was, 75 years later, at the bottom of the ocean, and brought up as one of the *Titanic*'s existing artifacts. And so Straithclyde's fine work was once again seen by the multitudes, and this was seen as an all-around victory for ocean-going cherubs.

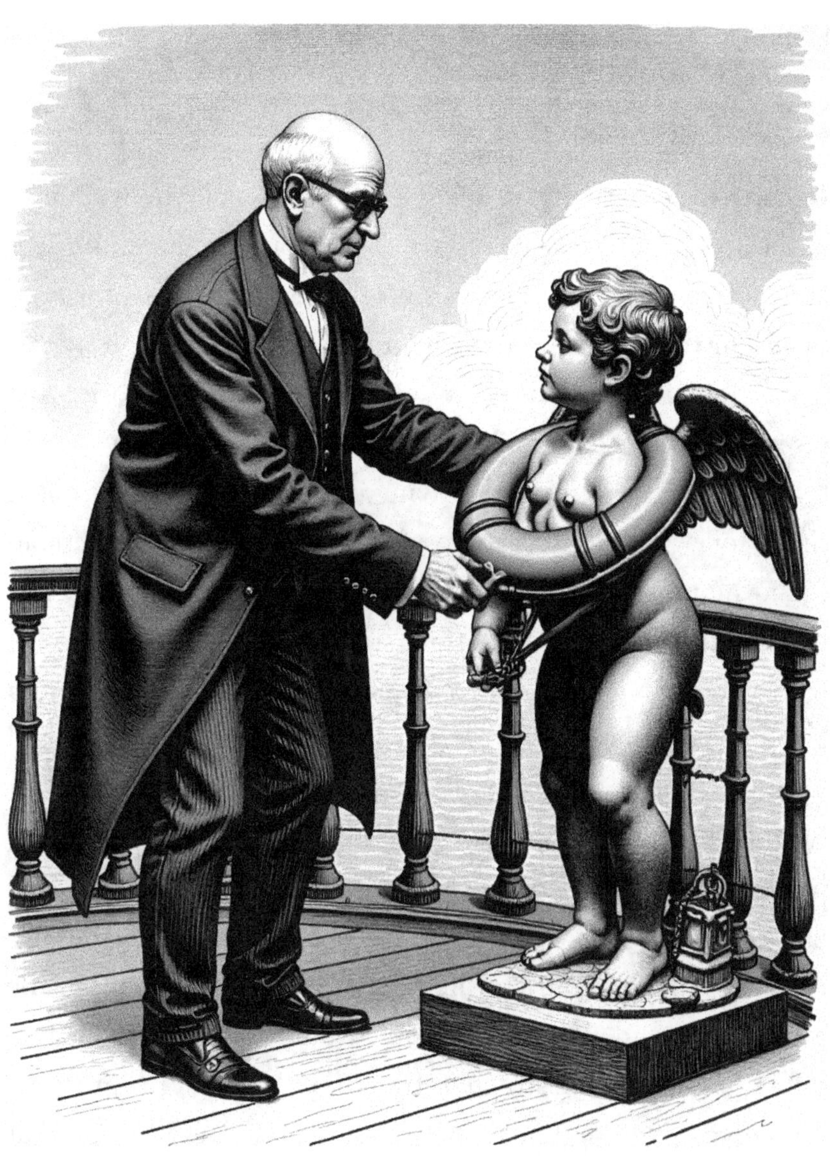

Warren Straithclyde and his beloved cherub.

---

(6) Sanford Waterman was a born salesman who won most of the special prizes that companies gave out to their employees as the "top salesman." It was said that Sanford was so good a salesman that he could "sell ice to Eskimos," although a later inspection of his meticulously kept records actually proved that his ice sales were extremely poor in the Inuit community.

One thing was for sure: Living in Belfast in 1910 was high times for a good lifeboat salesman, the very trade Waterman found himself in at that time. When the White Star Line was constructing *Titanic*, Waterman talked his way into project manager Thomas Andrews' office and managed to sell him on 20 lifeboats that could carry 1,178 people. This was still woefully short of covering the more than 2,200 passengers that would be sailing, but for mostly aesthetic reasons, the shipping line didn't want any more than that, despite Waterman's best efforts. Still, it was a real coup for Sanford because Andrews originally didn't want any lifeboats at all, as he figured, in the event of an accident, the rich people would probably just float to safety on crafts constructed from the bodies of third-class passengers. No one knows what was said in the office on that sales call, but Andrews was talked into five, and then 10, and, finally, 20 lifeboats in all. Perhaps Waterman had photos of Andrews with a woman other than his wife?

It should be said that Waterman was very fond of blackmail. He used his keen senses to look around the homes and businesses he'd sell to and find the right squeeze points, taking photos and collecting files like a private detective. Sanford could walk into any house, quickly size up the dark recesses, and come out with two sets of encyclopedias sold nearly every time. No one ever has bought two sets of encyclopedias from a principled salesman that refuses to use blackmail.

When Waterman won a free trip aboard the *Titanic* as a thanks for his sales figures, though, it was not the last time he was heard from. At that fateful hour, he actually talked his way into a lifeboat as the *Titanic* was sinking, under the guise that he would like to "monitor my lifeboats to see how they perform," and he was rescued the next morning by the *Carpathia* with the other passengers aboard lifeboat no. 12. Underneath the hand-scripted words "Lifeboat Performance," in his small notebook, though, were mostly just empty stick-figure scribblings and a picture of noted suffragette Emmeline Pankhurst drawn with enormous breasts.

The *Titanic* lifeboats did end up performing admirably on that night of danger, and it meant a huge surge in sales for the lifeboat company, but, ironically, the company, through a series of bad investments and a skimping on their normally high-quality building materials shortly thereafter, within a few years ended up underwater. And Waterman never again was able to sell, afterward, with quite the same ferocity, and shortly after the sinking, ended up only eighth in sales out of 10 for a company that sold novelty corncob pipes. Perhaps with the trauma he'd been through, he simply lost his taste for selling, and possibly also blackmail.

3

Nowadays, modern cruise ships dwarf the Titanic, *with the largest being about five times what* Titanic *weighed. But in 1912, the* Titanic *was the largest ship to ever set sail, at slightly over 882 feet in length, with over 46,000 gross tons in weight. But it still wasn't enough when nature challenged her to a duel in the North Atlantic.*

It was a duel that claimed more than 1,500 lives, including those who even may have perished well before the sinking took place.

(7) On that fateful night, a diminutive 38-year-old hatmaker from Birmingham, England, named **Britain Collings**, who was said by all accounts to be enormously intoxicated, claimed that he was constantly asking for his drinks "on the rocks" and being constantly disappointed in what he got in return. "Where is all the ice?" he wailed.

That all changed as he stood on the promenade deck along the right side of the ship, as it scraped along the side of the iceberg, sending pieces of ice careening onto multiple levels of the vessel. As ice began falling all around him, his wife, and his seven children, Collings was seen to extend his whiskey glass out in front of him, proclaiming, "Now that's more like it."

But that wasn't the end, for there was an exchange made. Pieces of ice fell onto the deck of the *Titanic,* and Collings, newly animated by the ice downpour, and with the overzealous, chance-taking bravado of a confident drunk man, suddenly hurled himself towards the boat's right-side railing, his drink in one hand, his walking cane in the other, and leapt clear over the railing and onto the enormous ice mass, landing on a lower shelf.

He was last heard shouting, "Oh, now I've gone and done it!" by his wife, who could only watch in helpless horror as the great ship sailed on.

And as she sat the next morning in the lifeboats with her newly fatherless brood of seven, she quietly vowed to a companion that she would not marry another hatmaker, for they were always "the wildest of men, unfit for fathering and unfit really, for anything other than the making of hats." And then, as if to refute even that point, the band on her Edwardian hat snapped off and fell determinedly into the sea.

---

(8) Although Britain Collings may have been one of the very first casualties of the *Titanic* accident, 42-year-old **Craddock Spahn** was the very first *confirmed* casualty. Having begun the new year of 1912 with a resolution to improve his well-being, Craddock vowed to cut down on the Lady Baltimore cakes and to exercise at almost every available opportunity. He also began to put leeches on his skin. Leeches had come back into fashion in the early 1910s as a weight loss curative because health professionals thought that leeches made you less hungry — which was probably true because they are pretty gross to look at and probably ruined a lot of people's appetites.

Craddock spent a lot of time in his cabin, lifting weights and doing a form of crunch exercise that's long been disavowed. He was not welcome into the first-class gym as a second-class passenger, and that was the only gym, so he turned his stateroom into a makeshift workout mecca, where he spent up to six hours a day sculpting himself into what would now be considered "thirst trap shape."

Craddock's untimely demise was actually discovered by a deckhand named Abe as he knocked on cabin doors on E deck, advising people to evacuate, 30 minutes after the iceberg grazing, and he found Craddock lying on his side, glassy-eyed, next to a pillow, with a probable neck break. Abe later testified that the fitness enthusiast was clad in a daringly skimpy exercise outfit and must have been balancing on his head when the ship hit, causing him to fall awkwardly.

In the end, Craddock Spahn was most probably casualty

number one — and with over two hours and 40 minutes of sinking yet to come, there would be many, many more.

---

(9) Myra Mattieu was what we would today call an influencer or a "self-absorbed pest with a camera." And the year 1912 was what made it all entirely possible, with the release of the innovative Vest Pocket Kodak. Before that, cameras were wooden, bulky, and foldable, but the new design permitted easy handheld use, and Myra discovered in her hometown of Toulouse, France, that she attracted attention with her snaps.

She found herself taking photos where she would spread her silken tresses across pillows, or sail on gentlemen's sailboats with the wind playing in her hair, and in some of her parlor shots, where repeated knee exposure made her the scandalous talk of the local region.

By the time she sailed on the *Titanic*, Myra had perfected 25 different poses, adjusting her neck position or the crook of her arm just so. Even walking up the gangplank with her photographer friend, Laurent, was an adventure of supple positioning and smiles, and she knew that men all around her were drawn to her enchanting ways with a substantial force. In fact, several husbands were slapped hard with silk fans and parasols by significant others not caught in her magnetic thrall but who understood what its power was capable of.

And on the ship, itself, as Myra led Laurent through a series of suggestive tableaux that had men near her tripping clumsily into doors and spilling full cups of coffee on their greatcoats, every day was an adventure. And the destination promised even more possibilities. The trip to New York City was to have found her with several appointments at many of the well-known local photography studios.

Myra, like Craddock Spahn, had her life force snuffed out just after 11:40 p.m. when the ship they were sailing upon rubbed against a solid object while it was traveling at just over 23 miles per hour. It was no more than a small jolt, but it was major to Laurent and Myra, who were engaging in the kind of daredevilry we know from watching videos of Russian kids hanging from high buildings. The two French adventurers were hanging from the back rail of the boat, trying to satisfy a young person's need to feel alive, and the jolt was enough to pry Myra loose and out into the water.

Laurent then climbed back over the rail in shock and instinctively felt for the Vest Pocket Kodak. It was still there, even if his muse was not. He recognized that she was gone and that he did not want to risk his own life to go back in after her, particularly in the very chic ensemble he was wearing. But he decided he would preserve the negatives as the only way to keep her still alive on the boat in the future.

Laurent, at the end, handed the camera to a young woman as she stepped into a lifeboat, gave her careful instructions on how to get the pictures printed and published, and then settled into one of the long, studied pouts that Myra had taught him.

Laurent, the innovative Vest Pocket Kodak, and Myra Mattieu.

4

Many of the world's richest and most famous people sailed on Titanic. *They went in excited as frolicking badgers, pressed shirts and ankle-length dresses on full display, ready to be a part of the experience. There were the famous names like Astor and Guggenheim, and Isidor Straus, the co-owner of Macy's. And just as many other famous people missed sailing on the* Titanic *for any number of reasons, even though they had tickets: Milton Hershey, the founder of Hershey's; the financier J.P. Morgan; and the author Theodore Dreiser, whose* An American Tragedy *had not yet been published and whose demise would have made that the* real *American tragedy.*

(10) Bosco Renfro, a first-class passenger, who was the U.S.'s initial importer of passion fruit to America, also sailed onboard the *Titanic*. Renfro had spent a good deal of time with his import/export business in southern Brazil looking for new discoveries to bring back, and when he found the passion fruit, he was enchanted. Just prior to sailing on *Titanic*, on a sales trip to Europe, he had successfully expanded his business, particularly in Spain and Italy, where calling something a "passion" fruit was like dropping pheromones from a hot-air balloon. He became the toast of that area as the "Passion Fruit King," and now, on his way back to America in triumph, Renfro could certainly have taken a smaller, less conspicuous vessel, but he wanted to bask in his success, and so he purchased a first-class cabin aboard the *Titanic* for himself and his dour wife, Malta. Ironically, despite all of his direct connections to passion fruit, he was in a particularly glum and loveless marriage.

During the crossing, Malta spent a lot of time reading in her cabin while Renfro shared his fruity find with the other first-class passengers. Nobody needed to settle for just simple lemons or cherries when Renfro was around, for passion fruit was always on the menu, and a lot of its juice ended up staining *Titanic* menus.

Sources say that Renfro was deep in heated disagreement with Malta while the ship struck something, suddenly silencing them. Within seconds, though, they were back at it, and Malta stormed out of the cabin and went outside and was rescued without ever saying farewell.

Renfro was last seen carrying a crate of what was most likely passion fruit down to the lower decks. His wife, in her memoir published eight years later, claimed that her husband sometimes had intercourse with the passion fruit while she sat by, idly turning the pages of a *Harper's Weekly*, and had stated that she would not be at all surprised if his last act on earth had involved copulation with the lusty fruit.

And there was an actual confirmation of this made 12 years post-memoir when a bottle washed up in Greenland in 1932 with a note inside, that finally made its way to his wife. The note was a final testament from Bosco to Malta, stating that he had known the ship was sinking, that he had no regrets about never finding and saying goodbye to her, and that he was going to spend his final moments with his beloved crate of passion fruits. At some point it was said that Malta placed the note back in the bottle, threw it into the fireplace, where it burned, and then pleasured herself with some Belgian endives. Turnabout, in that case, was fair play.

---

(11) There was a lot of old money from inherited wealth onboard the *Titanic*. But new money, or self-made fortunes, like Bosco Renfro's, were there as well. And they existed peacefully, if uneasily, side-by-side. The most famous of all of the self-mades was, of course, the "Unsinkable Molly Brown," who made her impression felt throughout the ship and later inside the lifeboats with her brusque energy and moral rectitude.

There was also **Horatio Weybridge.** Weybridge ran a chain of dry goods stores in Birmingham, England, and came on board with his mistress, Countess de Van der Jeet. Why the classy countess and Horatio Weybridge were an item, no one seemed to know. She was glamorous and well-heeled social royalty with a quick wit and an ongoing penchant for showing off her large collection of mink pelt wraps.

Countess de Van der Jeet, Frizz McCuddles, and some of her 15 mink pelts.

Horatio was seen as rather a dull fellow who often wore threadbare suits and punctuated his long, tedious speeches with occasional spitting off the side of the ship. And certainly James

Cameron was paying attention when he was trying to line up character traits for his *Titanic* film character, Jack Dawson.

Weybridge spit several hundred times off the ship during the trip, and at least three passengers reported being spit upon later, during the evacuation, as their lifeboats were being lowered into the sea.

At the end, Countess de Van der Jeet ended up escaping in the first launched lifeboat with a pile of 15 mink pelts and her yorkie, Frizz McCuddles. The staff of the ship, at those very early launches, had not yet set limits on the space used for things, if there was extra space in the lifeboats, and one woman even brought with her six hat boxes and a life-size mannequin.

In the end, most of Countess de Van der Jeet's pelts survived, but Horatio Weybridge did not. He bid the countess farewell, helped her with the pelt transfer to the lifeboat, and then died honorably, drinking and spitting off the side of the ship like a turbo-charged baseball player.

Five days later, 306 bodies were gathered in on the main retrieval mission undertaken by the SS *Mackay-Bennett* to find and recover bodies from the *Titanic*. Weybridge's was among the bodies found, frozen like an unopened package of fish sticks, with a spittle wad frozen in the corner of his mouth, aimed at eternity.

---

(12) Mrs. Evelyn Pennyspancer was a rich widow from Baltimore whose husband, Sterling, had inherited all of his wealth from his father, and who before that had inherited wealth from his father, the founder of the Pennyspancer legacy. The Pennyspancers were on the cutting edge of fake hair technology, and their latest snappable long-wearer had been selling extremely well in the early 1910s.

Evelyn noted that there were many, many wearers of Pennyspancer products in first class on the *Titanic*, and, if they knew who she was, would greet her on deck with a subtle, conspiratorial head nod. Evelyn, for her own daily amusement, would bring a topped-off glass of expensive champagne down to the lower decks to drink in a corner and then throw a Pennyspancer hairpiece onto a table and watch as the rabble fought over it, chuckling as they invariably tore the hair swatch to pieces.

When the ship began to sink, she was placed in *Titanic*'s lifeboat no. 6, just behind the "Unsinkable Molly Brown," and when Brown began her entreaties to turn around and pick up some of the passengers from the water, Evelyn Pennyspancer is reported to have said, "Oh, no, you don't, you new-monied cow," and to have struck her firmly about the head and shoulders with a small clutch of wig pieces in her possession.

Evelyn Pennyspancer died a widow in 1940, at the age of 77, safe and comfortable at home on a soft, downy bed made of human hair.

5

There was a total of 908 crew members on the Titanic, *317 of whom worked with the engineering crew belowdecks in the heat with the 29 boilers and 162 coal-burning furnaces that made the tireless ship go. There were engineers, electricians, stokers who kept the fires going, greasers who oiled all the machines, and coal trimmers who controlled the smooth flow of coal to all the furnaces. And of these 317 men, only 72 survived.*

(13) One of those who made it through was **Hugh Allslop**, a 19-year-old greaser. What greasers meant in the 1950s obviously was very different from what a greaser was back in 1912. While '50s greasers slicked back their hair and sang about summer romances and got into knife fights with the "socs," 1912 greasers were the merchant seamen who kept all the engines on ocean liners well-lubricated. Their "summer nights" were spent doing the difficult, low-paying, and thankless work they did, but their jobs were essential. "Walla-walla-walla." And they were not likely to be wearing cool-looking leather jackets while they were baking belowdecks in the sweltering heat.

Allslop was born in Southampton, England, where much of the engineering crew on the *Titanic* was from. He was fascinated by oil and grease from a very young age, and his family even had its own barrel of oil inexplicably standing inside the entrance of its brick row home. No one could really remember how the oil barrel ended up there, but it allowed young Hugh to stretch his interest in lubrication from a passing fancy into a steady obsession. He was often seen at home in his youth oiling the wheel hinges on his toy wagon or sticking his arms shoulder-deep into the murky liquid just for something to play with. He was sometimes referred to by neighbors as "that right-odd oil kid." So it was no surprise when ship work came calling that he was there on the other end to answer the call. He climbed inside the bowels of that ship and did his work to the best of his abilities.

Greasers generally worked a four-hours-on, four-hours-off schedule, and Allslop had come off his round at exactly 10 p.m. that fateful evening. A little later, as he was collecting scraps of onion to make a simple soup, he recalled there was a bump, saying it felt just like "a lubricated engine coughing out a bit of oil." It was an extremely strange way to describe what he had heard, but no follow-up questions were asked.

Allslop made his way to the back railing of the ship as it

began its final descent into the ocean, and he was a champion hanger who would not be easily shaken. He claims the next thing he remembers was going under and then quickly resurfacing and pretending that the water was lukewarm oil, so that he wouldn't be overwhelmed by its frigidity. He was rescued by one of the few lifeboats to come back, with one passenger claiming they "found him in his own little world and hallucinating," which, really, was not all that dissimilar to his normal mindstate.

Shortly after the rescue, Allslop was back at sea — to the life he knew and loved — but every time he came to the family home, people always made sure that barrel of oil was waiting for him, to greet him like an old, faithful friend.

He was eventually laid to rest in an oil barrel at an open barrel ceremony and buried in Southampton Cemetery in 1945, a life of slick and responsible hard work lived to its fullest.

---

(14) Peter Cleaves was an electrician on the ship who may or may not have died in the disaster; no one knows for sure. All that was certain was that a small and pale 20-year-old man named Peter Cleaves, with soft features and the barest wisp of a mustache, went onboard the ship as an electrician in Southampton and that a woman named Susan Jones, in a flower-patterned dress, with soft features and the barest wisp of a female mustache, left the ship on lifeboat no. 14 at 1:25 a.m. on that ominous night.

Cleaves was born into the unluckiest family in Liverpool in 1892, the 21st of 22 children, 18 of whom had died in childhood. He learned the electrician trade from his two older brothers, who went on to work for the railroad. But Peter had a dream one night in which the train he was on derailed and steamed ahead into a lake and somehow just kept going. The next day, Peter mentioned to his family his desire to work out at sea, much to the chagrin of his two railroad brothers, who reportedly boxed his ears until they cauliflowered.

Most of his work movements were kept track of on board the ship, but no one knows where Peter went after the ship hit the iceberg. He may well have died that night with the other seven electricians aboard. It is actually to the electricians' great credit that, in the two hours and 40 minutes between the strike and the sinking, they kept the power on the ship working until the very last few minutes. But was it possible that Peter Cleaves abandoned his post after the accident and spent his time going through abandoned cabins, grabbing tasteful wardrobe and makeup items, only to remake himself into someone new?

In the inquiry held shortly after the sinking, the woman calling herself Susan Jones was made to testify, since she was not on any passenger manifest. Susan claimed that she was a stowaway who snuck onto the boat at Southampton. She reported that she variously stayed in different sections of the ship and counted on kind, single gentlemen in first and second class to let her stay in their cabins. It was noted by a court reporter of the day that, though Susan looked and sounded very feminine and claimed to be a schoolteacher, her hands had the rough-hewn look of a manual laborer.

In the end, checkmate, Peter Cleaves, if he did indeed become a woman, because he lived alone in Southampton for the rest of his life as Susan Jones. And whether he ever really told anyone of the Mrs. Doubtfire he may have pulled, no one officially came forward.

Susan Jones lived for 62 more years after the *Titanic* disaster and died in her bed, and even though there was the legend that had sprung up, the funeral director considered it indiscreet to check Susan Jones' genitalia at the end since she had not died under suspicious circumstances. So the possible mystery was never resolved. And whether the sinking of the mighty ship into the cold Atlantic waters that night had turned a man "gender fluid," no one could really say for sure.

---

(15) Roderick Evans was a meticulous employee of the White Star Line who worked belowdecks and was responsible for the safe passage of cargo from his small office in the cargo hold. The heavy packages, steamer trunks, and even a car were kept there. Because the car was in a crate, though, it's highly unlikely that any amorous couple could have had steamy sex in the back seat or really anywhere in a cargo hold manned by Roderick Evans. His was a spotless chamber of which he knew every inch, and he patrolled and catalogued it to the letter.

Roderick Evans, cargo.

Passengers who occasionally walked down to the cargo hold to "check on their things" (wink) dealt with the smart, crystalline mind of its protector — a man who knew what couples with flushed expressions and nervous impatience were up to. Invariably, they wished to have sex in a quiet, out-of-the-way place, even if it was on pieces of rope and sailcloth. But, alas, Evans was very wise to all of these machinations, and the few times he did catch a couple having sex after they had cleverly slipped past him, he did not let it continue, instead separating them with an enormous anus-inserted rubber grappling hook he had fashioned for just such a purpose.

Evans himself was unmarried and thought to have not gotten very much, if any, sex in his lifetime. Some said perhaps that was what caused him to fastidiously separate others from the act with his anti-sex hook. Whatever the case, no one can clearly recall having seen Evans on deck that night after the iceberg struck. It is believed that he probably stayed below in his office the whole time, trusty hook by his side, protecting his cargo hold until the end, to finally perish in a cold, quiet, non-sexual way — a simple finish some believed would have been much to his liking.

6

Not everyone on the Titanic *was human. There was a canary, some roosters, a ship's cat that reportedly left before the ship set sail from Southampton with a litter of newborn kittens in tow, plenty of rats — probably more so after the cat left — and 12 dogs, among others. And out of the dozen canines, only three survived the trip — small ones saved by their compactness — as their first-class owners quietly tucked them into warm pieces of clothing. It was a fate not shared with the larger breeds, however. They were not allowed onto the lifeboats and, because of it, perished — hopefully all the while remaining "good boys" and "good girls."*

(16) *Titanic* ship steward **Felton Steward** actually became a steward because his Dad was a steward, and he thought, as a boy, people just became whatever their names were. But when he found out that a local tavern owner in his hometown was named Joseph Blacksmith, it shattered his worldview entirely.

Felton became a steward on the *Titanic* at 19 years of age and was assigned to animal duty. All of the pets brought along by passengers fell under his dominion, and he would make sure every animal had enough food and water, that they weren't tearing up the boat furnishings, and that they stayed out of the first-class punch bowls.

The majority of the dogs stayed in the kennels located on F deck, and they were let out, walked daily, and allowed to do their business by Felton Steward on the poop deck, a name which was, in this case, entirely justified. Most of the dogs were well-behaved, although one dog named Willoughby was said to have jumped up playfully onto a first-class passenger named Stanton and duly received a sharp crack on the snout with Stanton's walking stick. Willoughby reportedly retaliated later by chewing on Stanton's hands while he was dangling from the ship, after Steward probably let the dogs go free from their kennels near the end so they at least had a fighting chance. People also recall seeing Steward, during the sinking, on deck, affixing custom-made life-rings to as many of the pets as he could find. Yes, even the parrots.

In the end, Steward's body was found five days afterward, floating in the North Atlantic, by the salvage ship SS *Mackay-Bennett*. He was given a hero's burial in Halifax, Nova Scotia, and the hole he was placed in was prepared by two workers, named Paul Graves and Thomas Digger.

---

(17) Second-class passenger **Stormont McKeever** was always seen on deck with a macaw named Sterling on his shoulder, firmly gripping the tweed fabric there and repeating the things Stormont said. By his fourth year of bird ownership, though, Stormont had learned not to speak too loudly if he didn't want an immediate, clear-voiced recitation of his comments bursting out of his avian friend. As a frequent wearer of cravats, the necktie's older cousin, Stormont had, at the time, become quite the fashion critic on the wearing of cravats, and his macaw several times repeated his disapproving comments as his high, reedy-voiced double.

McKeever would often go for long, drawn-out visits to the upper decks alone to spy on and critique the cravats there and was surprised to find that the first-class passengers were often quite sloppy in their cravat prep. Perhaps the small bits of "miscare" were the work of the first-class passengers' servants' small rebellions or perhaps first-class men pulled at their cravats all too frequently until they became misshapen.

During his solo walking tours, Stormont would often lodge his macaw in the F deck kennels with the nice young ship's steward, Felton Steward. Steward had a couple of spare cages and seemingly endless stores of lettuce and seeds. And always, at the end of the day, it would take Sterling at least 10 minutes to stop barking like a dog — which he would pick up from the other noisy lodgers each time — and resume normal conversation, as Stormont and Sterling would proceed directly to their cabin. And if you'd have walked by the cabin just a bit after that, you would have heard a macaw excitedly repeating pointed reviews of shipmates' cravats.

Sterling and Stormont spent four happy days together on board the *Titanic*. By day three, Stormont had also taught his pet macaw to nod in greeting, a polite gesture they did in tandem as they passed people, and it made the duo a hit on board the ship. And when they went to bed at 11 p.m. on that fourth night, they had just gotten pre-prepped for another pleasant time out in the salty air for what would be the following day. But just over a half hour later, the ship wobbled a bit, sending Sterling off his perch and directly into a busy round of squawking. Cravat reviews became the farthest thing from the duo's thinking from then on.

Heading for the top deck, Stormont picked out a life vest for himself, and as Felton Steward was handing out the custom vests he made for the animals, Sterling the macaw was seen refusing it. The bird would take its chances clinging tenaciously to one of the shoulders of Stormont's life jacket, and that was that.

No one knows how Stormont McKeever made it into the water, but his body was found five days later by the salvage ship SS *Mackay-Bennett*, not far from Felton Steward, coincidentally, and there, half-frozen but still alive on his stiff shoulder was Sterling, confused, pacing weakly, and repeating the words: "That's a poorly assembled cravat, Felton. I'm gonna die in this frozen soup and I've never even been to Krakow."

Stormont McKeever, second-class passenger. Sterling, macaw

---

(18) Jack Dawson, Leonardo DiCaprio's character from the movie *Titanic*, may actually have been based on a dog named Porslikken. The term "comfort animal" didn't exist in those days, but this wetterhoun, or Dutch water dog, served that purpose in 1912, providing excellent solace to his female master, 28-year-old **Lotte Janssen**, whose husband had recently perished in the Netherlands in a tulip farming accident.

Lotte had sold off the tulip farm not long after the incident and was sailing to America to go live with relatives in southwestern Minnesota. Since Lotte had not had children, Porslikken was her whole world now, and she treated him as almost more human than dog. Bones that she gave to Porslikken were from the finest reindeer thighs, and she often had Porslikken dine with her in her stateroom wearing a tux-and-bib combo.

Another second-class passenger and fellow Dutch resident also headed to America, Lucas Visser, was said to have formed a fast bond with her and may have possibly asked for her hand in marriage on day three, but Lotte may not have been ready for the married life again so soon. Also, some believe that Porslikken disapproved.

Felton Steward, the ship's steward-slash-dog keeper, would stop in every day at 2 p.m. and walk Porslikken for Lotte while she took her 45-minute nap. The dog would be led along excitedly about the ship, and then, some said, stand behind Steward and rear up on its hind legs whenever they got to the bow of the boat, as if their spirits were taking flight.

On the night of the sinking, after Porslikken was drawn into his life preserver by Steward on deck, and Lotte began heading for a lifeboat, picking up her furry, mid-sized friend to place inside, one of the boat staff informed her that no dogs were allowed in the boats. But rather than leave him behind, Lotte chose to remain with Porslikken on deck and take her chances there.

Lotte later told the story of how she traveled down into the deep, gripping the *Titanic*'s railing, but that just before they went under, Porslikken barked loudly and repeatedly, and it inspired her to kick toward the surface. When they got there, it was chaos, but Porslikken began biting the arms of people that were clambering over Lotte in a panic in the water, and the dog then helped his master up onto a wooden piece of door framing. Porslikken tried to clamber up too, but it seemingly threatened to topple the makeshift raft, so he stayed there, paws up on the wood as the rest of his body dangled in the frigid water.

Lotte also spoke of how Porslikken had died in that position, but that his inspiring barks played over and over in her mind, and she determined that she must get to safety and then go on and keep living. As she undid Porslikken's frozen paws from the wooden edifice and watched him quietly float away into the deep, she began paddling until she spotted a rescue lifeboat that had turned around to help the very few that were still alive. Endless speculation later centered around the fact that maybe the dog could have also fit on that giant piece of wood with Lotte, but a consensus was never reached.

Later, as Lotte stood on the deck of the *Carpathia*, tired, cold, and wrapped in a shawl, Dutchman Lucas Visser was seen walking through. He had somehow survived and was searching for someone. But Lotte sunk her head into her shawl and quietly receded into a corner and, she never saw Lucas again. She died 72 years later while holding Porslikken's dog collar in her hand.

7

The Titanic *was a luxury hotel to some and a bargain-basement Econo Lodge to others. And the luxurious aspects of first class didn't just end with the well-ordered staterooms, a first-rate gym, a smoking room, and a special reading and writing room. There was also plenty to eat in the dining saloon, café, and a fancy restaurant called The Ritz.*

The Ritz employed 68 people — the majority from Italy and France — and they prepared and delivered some of the most sumptuous meals on Earth to the hungry first-class passengers. And even if the well-heeled rich people treated them with less respect than they deserved, still, they refused to drop bugs into their food; it was the maiden voyage after all, and the staff wanted everything to be perfect. The bugs could wait until the first return voyage back across the Atlantic.

The Ritz operated from 8 a.m. to 11 p.m. daily, and tables were almost always fully booked. But only the manager of The Ritz was an employee of the White Star Line. The other 67 people were hired as independent contractors by that manager, Luigi Gatti. This peculiarity led to their later being shunted to one side as gig workers often are, when the lifeboats were filling, and as a result 64 of the 67 ultimately perished. The only survivors were two women who were allowed to eventually board a lifeboat and a kitchen clerk named Paul Maugé, who jumped into one of the boats as it was being lowered, breaking both legs of the woman he jumped onto.

(19) Emile Donnault's official title was wine butler, but today we would call him a "sommelier" or a "wild wine slinger." Donnault was a Frenchman from Le Havre who was a sophisticate when it came to movement and color, and he had a sparkling — yes, that's a pun — sense of humor. Whenever someone asked him everything he did as a wine butler, he would invariably answer, "I would like to tell you, but I decant." Monied audiences in that era would invariably laugh and expel fine vintages through their noses in violent, happy surprise at the response, and Donnault actually held a small, special handkerchief in his pocket for the nose messes that resulted.

Donnault was visited in Le Havre by Luigi Gatti one day late in 1911 at the restaurant where he worked, The Jazzbound Snail, when Gatti was scouting for the "absolute best wine butler in all of France." This was in the days long before reality show competitions, when potential seekers of talent had to jump into horse-drawn carriages and travel hundreds of miles to hunt down their quarry. Gatti had just visited another potential wine butler in a café outside of Le Havre but found his pouring technique a little stiff and amateurish and his verbal manner a tad pitchy. He was hoping for an improvement at Donnault's interview and was not disappointed.

Donnault zipped around The Jazzbound Snail like a graceful elk, and wine bottles were judiciously opened with a rhythmic precision, his wine napkin draped expertly on his forearm, sense of humor ready to fire. The never-fail "decant joke" most likely sealed the *Titanic* position for Donnault, which he recorded later in his personal diary:

> "Diary, I think I may just be the greatest living comedian in the world, as my customers can attest, and my greatest joke seems to have landed me a job this day on the world's biggest and most heralded ship, *Titanic*. My comedy is ready to set sail. Ha-ha, and I've gone and done it again just now."

Donnault reported for duty on April 10th in Cherbourg, France, the boat's first of two local stops before heading out across the ocean, and he was fully prepared to dazzle all comers. He would gladly have soaked himself daily in wine on the boat, if asked, but he had an abject fear of water, even going so far as to stay away from the rails on all the decks when he went out walking between shifts.

When the ship hit the iceberg, Donnault felt the bump in his cabin and had a premonition that this meant something very bad. But he wouldn't go anywhere near the water that night – if fate willed it, the water would have to come to him.

He rushed to the restaurant, already closed, and surrounded himself with wine bottles, sources say. He opened a few of the bottles and began expertly pouring himself drink after drink, robust reds and silky whites all disappearing in quick succession.

After the sinking, Emile Donnault's wine-marinated body was never found, but when Robert Ballard's crew searched the *Titanic* in 1986, one year after its discovery, a small remotely operated vehicle entered the place where the first-class restaurant had once been and found these words crudely carved into the wall in a messy, drunken hand: "You want me to explain what happened to the *Titanic*, but I decant."

---

(20) Italian-born **Benito Bianchi** was the head pastry chef at The Ritz on *Titanic*. Bianchi was recruited from the same restaurant as Emile Donnault in Le Havre, and it was quite a coup. The Jazzbound Snail instantly lost one of the world's best wine butlers, if not comedians, and one of the very best pastry chefs, and its reputation subsequently suffered greatly as a result.

Bianchi was born in 1872 in a small village outside of Naples, the year after the final year of a tradition that dated back to the Roman era, The Blood Cull. Held each June on the first day of summer in his village, all newborns were to be brought to the city square in the town proper and placed on an altar shaped like an enormous pizza tray. Two of the newborns were then chosen at random to be sacrificed each year — often picked out if they cried — and their blood was used in the pizza sauce for the celebration later that night. Bianchi was probably lucky the tradition had ended the year before his birth because he was a temperamental crier as a baby, and that would have put a big target on his forehead during the Blood Cull.

As an adult, Bianchi remained very whiny and temperamental, but his desserts were always top-notch. His crème brûlée was absolutely to die for, and a number of people who ate it on the *Titanic* did, in fact, end up dying. (Not from the crème brûlée though, obviously.)

Bianchi lived in a small hovel in Le Havre with a tiny kitchen that was stuffed with his cooking medals and covered in flour, but his pastry kitchen on the *Titanic* was generously appointed in the space that was afforded him to work his culinary magic. And Bianchi was a bona fide star on the boat. People often sent him notes in his kitchen as he cooked, praising his way with chocolate, and demanding that he work at their garden parties in Newport, Rhode Island, or The Caymans (in its pre-concealing-money period).

The great Benito Bianchi, pastry chef.

During the evacuation of *Titanic*, Bianchi stood at the lifeboats in his distinctive pastry garb, rocking back and forth on his heels, handing the departing passengers his famous butterscotch cookies, and the female passengers in first class pleaded with the ship's officers that he be placed in a boat — but an earlier prank on some of the officers, where he filled their hats with Baked Alaska, now came back to haunt him at this critical time.

The great Benito Bianchi, knowing the end was near, was seen stuffing himself with leftover cookies and then jumping without a life jacket into the water before the ship went under, and the dessert bar was officially closed.

---

(21) Tino Salmonetti was a 22-year-old waiter from Pisa who was great at his job but also a fast talker who played loosely with the truth and was full of bluster and braggadocio. He was picked for the job for his English skill, his smooth efficiency with plates and linens and had a precise, elephant-like memory for food orders. When he started telling customers that competing sets of his relatives worked on the restoration of the famed tower centuries ago in his hometown of Pisa, and that one set of his relatives got mad at the other and begin pounding on one end of the tower all night long, one evening, it started to strain believability. People loved the food at The Ritz, and the Pisa-born waiter was charming, but they began to grow skeptical that the man's relatives had created the tower's lean.

Surviving customers also recalled Salmonetti talking about an uncle who controlled the water levels in the Venice canals, and that if the city failed to properly compensate him on a monthly basis — which it habitually did — he would drastically lower the water in all the canals and disrupt the city's tourism.

He also claimed to have once found a secret room in the Roman Colosseum that no one else knew about and to have nearly drowned in the Trevi Fountain when he slipped on some coins.

When the *Titanic* hit the iceberg, he was likely smoking in bed and reading a tabloid newspaper, perhaps gathering new tales to tell, as he usually did every night after his shift ended, but no one ever recalled seeing him again.

That doesn't stop members of Salmonetti's family from boasting about him to this day. Some claim he saved a lot of people on the *Titanic* that night by jumping on and untangling ropes that had gotten stuck around a bunch of the lifeboats that were being lowered, while others claim he stayed with the captain of the ship until it sank, assuring him that the accident was not his fault. Whatever the case, the creator of legends had himself become a piece of *Titanic*'s legend: a "legendee," if you will – which is a word that Salmonetti claimed in his journals to have invented for himself during the Italo-Turkish War the year prior after saving an entire platoon of men.

8

The Titanic *disaster, like any other untoward event in history, was subject to its legends, its lore, and its conspiracies and myth-making, a lot of which was simply untrue. For instance,* Titanic *was never really described as "unsinkable" beforehand – that was first mentioned as someone's opinion the day after the sinking in the* New York Times *. And also, journalist Nellie Bly's assertion that there was a murderous clown moving among the passengers, quietly waiting until the cloak of night to feed on human flesh, was also quietly shot down, and the clown community still repeatedly denies it.*

(22) Penfold Whitacre, a 70-year-old man haunted by the death of his young wife, Sarah, in childbirth two months earlier, claimed that her brooding ghost was there with him on board the *Titanic*. Whitacre had also been taking a whole host of drugs to deal with the loss of his beloved and was spotted on deck several times having seizures. The medications he was taking were likely giving him hallucinations as well, since medications in the 1910s were mostly side effects, and his key enablers — his personal porter, Stanley, and his manservant, Charles — likely fed into his "visions," since their salaries were paid by Whitacre, and they told him what he wanted to hear. For instance, one passenger overheard Whitacre brokenly say, "The ghost of my dearly departed follows me continually," and instead of trying to quietly ignore or discourage that kind of thinking, manservant Charles was heard to say, "Yes, sir, she has been trailing behind you closely like a wedding train."

Anyone who knew the happy couple from their two-and-a-quarter years of wedded bliss knew that he had a rare and beautiful connection with his wife despite their nearly 50-year age difference, perhaps because they were related by blood. Whatever it was, this connection seemed to have survived her death.

On the night of the sinking, Whitacre was seen out late alone "accompanying" his wife placidly on a deckside stroll. As confused passengers looked on in concern, Whitacre seemed to be both calmly talking to as well as answering an invisible person's questions. And just before the mighty ship tore along the iceberg, a ship's psychiatrist had been summoned by one of the ship's crew to talk to him.

Penfold Whitacre and his ghost wife, Sarah.

The psychiatrist, a Dr. Mark Cleminger, may have spoken to Whitacre a bit, but whatever he told him has been lost to the ages, as both men perished in the icy Atlantic. Whitacre was last seen sliding down the deck while holding onto the air in front of him. And in his mind, the grabbed space was most likely occupied by his astonishingly young soulmate, Sarah, and it could be credibly claimed that they died in each other's arms that night, even though her ghost would certainly have been eligible for a seat in a lifeboat.

---

(23) There was talk on the ship that a scientist onboard, **Dr. Emile Krenhertz**, kept a preserved body in a wooden box in the cargo hold. Krenhertz told people who asked about it that it was a body that had been donated in London for medical study, that had been boxed up and preserved for the voyage back to the States. But a rumor soon began, most likely within a group that was headed to America to attend an underground conference, that the body was being used to reanimate dead tissue. The group in question was the Mary Shelley Society, so you can see why those people would have been especially sensitive to the matter.

The Mary Shelley Society was a paranoid conspiracy group made up of nine men and one woman, and they were seen often on the promenade deck sitting in chairs in a semi-circle in their gloomy, dark clothing, ears pricked up like antennae, paying close attention to everything around them. When Penfold

Whitacre passed them one evening, "talking to his ghost wife," they were his only boatmates not inclined to make fun or be alarmed.

Roger Tower, the leader of the Mary Shelley Society, overheard Dr. Krenhertz talking about his profession with an astonished society lady, and he quickly reported it back to his clique. A scientist simply accounting for the day-to-day in his medical studies soon quickly blossomed into a full-bore theory complete with devious motives and unnatural desires. It didn't help that Dr. Krenhertz had an eye patch, the result of an unfortunate clarinet incident from when he was a child. The Mary Shelley Society had its red meat, and now it was time to feast.

That fourth night on the ship, Roger Tower and his group gathered and divided up tasks. One segment of the group was to penetrate the cargo hold and destroy the body used for the doctor's "cursed" experiments; another was to confront the evil doctor and make him confess; a third group was to alert the leadership on the boat and explain the situation to them, in the fervent hope that they would clap the doctor in irons.

And at just after 11:30 p.m., they gathered on deck to go over their plans. As they were finalizing it all, the boat bumped into the block of ice, which deposited smaller pieces of ice onto the deck and onto the black cloaks they were wearing. The Mary Shelley Society immediately turned its attention instead to a new purpose, because they knew the ship would sink — they just *knew it* — and so ran for the lifeboats, and quickly.

Unfortunately, conspiracy theorists, then as now, see very little actual daylight and usually neglect basic eating and exercise regimens, so even though most of them tried getting into the lifeboats, they were easily kept out by much stronger, fitter men. The one woman in the society, Sadie Tristance, received a spot in a lifeboat and was eventually charged with telling the group's heroic story so it would not be lost to time. She promised to tell all of America about the heroism of the Mary Shelley Society and how they stopped an inhuman beast, made from scattered parts, from being born. This beast, they theorized, would have wandered the length and breadth of the country, murdering people. At the same time, they had stopped its mad scientist creator from escaping the boat.

Dr. Krenhertz's research was thusly lost to time. When a couple members of the Mary Shelley Society finally caught up with him, they were spotted throwing him overboard into the frigid water with all of his notes that he held in a satchel by his side. And so his research on insulin was gone, and sufferers would have to wait another 10 years before they could get relief for their diabetes.

And Sadie Tristance wrote her book about the Mary Shelley Society, which found a bigger publisher than expected, because of the *Titanic* angle, but it was quickly dismissed by critics and the buying public because it was plagued with repetitive, lunatic, manifesto-like storytelling, and, also, because a book published a year earlier by a colleague of Dr. Krenhertz had countered what the Mary Shelley Society had to say about the doctor and eloquently made the case that the doctor was a kind man who wanted to help people. And so Sadie joined the fringe lecture circuit, largely peopled by charlatans, mystics, and disgraced physicians, and would go underground afterward and only raise her head occasionally during her long life to comment on things like the Lindbergh baby kidnapping or Area 51.

Sadie, at the end, suffered a debilitating stroke in 1967 and died two years later, on July 20, 1969, minutes before the lunar module touched down on the moon for the first time. Others of her ilk would then be forced to carry the conspiracy banner in challenging the efficacy of the moon mission, as poor Sadie Tristance was no longer around to obsessively care.

---

(24) Diederik Hansen was a Danish spiritualist sailing in first class, because spiritualism was big business at the time, and top spiritualists could command very good money pretending to communicate with the dead. Hansen was on his way to give a lecture series at venues on the east coast of America, discussing his new theory that 50% of the dead "come back" because they want to ride in a horse and buggy just one more time. And he claimed to have ridden along with many souls to their final rest, sometimes using his very own horse and buggy "packed tightly with up to five specters."

On a deck of the *Titanic* as it sailed, and after the sun would set, Hansen would set out a few lanterns and ply first-class passengers with private spiritual readings. The people in first-class, especially the old money ones, were less likely to embrace death, since they didn't want to believe they could die and lose all their money. Their concerns were mostly about that when they were contacting their relatives. They wanted to feel that their parents and grandparents or their fellow private social club members who'd passed on before them were somehow transcending death and being treated as the pampered supreme beings they were on Earth, sipping port and being attended to by the many people beneath them in life.

And Hansen did not disappoint them with his findings. He told Benjamin Guggenheim that his grandfather was living on a palm-tree-lined island in the afterlife being fanned by a ghost manservant named Montague. And John Jacob Astor IV was assured, with Hansen acting as a mouthpiece, that his family had not only gone into "the light" that escorted them all into the afterlife, but were now the majority owners of "the light" and were making each subsequently deceased person pay a percentage of their "soul points" just to be let in.

Hansen also turned into another enabler of Penfold Whitacre, whose wife Hansen "saw" roaming the decks of the mighty ship. When Whitacre wanted to know why his ghost wife had followed him onto the ship, Hansen reportedly told him that she wanted a last sail with him. This was a variant on Hansen's "last horse and buggy ride" story, and it seemed to relax Whitacre. Whitacre no longer was haunted by his wife and began to "accompany her" on strolls and chat happily with her.

In the end Hansen was last spotted on the deck of the *Titanic* after the crash late that night, deep into a whiskey bottle, trying to "talk to the spirits," while accepting very large sums of cash from men in fine clothes who needed assurance that their afterlife was secure. Perhaps he thought by keeping busy, he wouldn't have to concentrate so much on the creaks and the water rise that was making their demises all but assured. But soon enough, both he and his lanterns slid down the deck, as he cried out to the spirits he claimed to have contacted, and into whatever oblivion that awaited them.

Stories of Hansen's trained apprentice spiritualist— a man named Charlton – who had stayed behind in Denmark instead of sailing on the *Titanic*, were written about in the pre-eminent spiritualist publications of the time. Charlton claimed to have contacted the spirit of Hansen a few days after the *Titanic*'s fatal plunge and that Hansen told him what he wanted just once more: a horse and buggy ride.

Oh, and also for Charlton to get absolutely all of Hansen's inheritance. "I want Charlton to become fabulously wealthy," Charlton claimed his mentor's spirit had said, and that settled the matter with the local authorities at the time, who were an especially superstitious lot. Spiritual wishes had been conveyed, and Charlton retired to a castle in the Rhine Valley in the Northern region of Germany and raised bats.

9

Wallace Hartley was a conductor and violinist, a veteran of 80 maritime voyages, who led a group of seven other classical musicians on board, most famously on the fateful night of the Titanic's *plunge, when all eight decided to gallantly play as the ship began to sink, to try and calm the nerves of the people despite their hopeless situation. None of the eight survived.*

But they were far from the only artists on board.

(25) Frenchman **Jacques Duhaime** was a 32-year-old mime who boarded the *Titanic* in Cherbourg and began to entertain passengers right from the start with his specialty bits: the "Strong Wind Pushing Against You," the "Man Stuck in the Box," and the then-popular "Giraffe in Oil-Soaked Pajamas."

Jacques Duhaime. Mime.

This was during the golden era of the mime, one in which a top mime could fill a 5,000-seat venue and elicit gales of laughter with his miming routines. Times were much simpler, and mimes were major celebrities. Duhaime was hired by a French entertainment company in Paris and was considered to be one of the top three mimes in his *arrondissement*. He came on board and performed with gusto, delighting the first- and second-class passengers, sometimes in accompaniment with the ship's band, and passengers commented often on how he injected real honesty into his routines. He would find himself stuck definitively in the imaginary box with such conviction, for instance, that claustrophobia sufferers would immediately lapse into panic attacks right there in front of him.

When he wasn't miming, Duhaime could usually be found running in the ship's first-class gymnasium or on one of the aft decks, limbs as light as air. And he had an impressive runner's build, especially for a man who as a child had survived diphtheria, pneumonia, whooping cough, enteritis, scarlet fever, tuberculosis, and cholera.

In the end, Duhaime was a steadfast man, bold and brave, and he decided to join the band on deck one last time on the night of the sinking, performing his mime routines next to them as the ship took on water and began to slowly list to one side. The few survivors that remember seeing him remarked that he could have probably dived in and swam strongly to a lifeboat to save himself, but he committed to his routines, so much so that when the ship began pointing heavily downward, he didn't grab onto a railing as one might do, but instead attempted to do the

"Pulling the Invisible Rope" thing to hoist himself back up the deck, which was all to no avail, naturally. It was a final look at the dedication and devotion to his craft right before he met an icy end. Later, people also remarked that when he hit the water, he did not cry out from the shock of the cold or the pain — he stayed completely silent. It was an honorable death for a mime.

---

(26) Milla Franks was a self-proclaimed "dancer of substance and refinement," who might have made a large city's ballet company if she hadn't become so very fond of saloon dancing. Eventually, she become known to time as the "Disaster Black Widow" after three of her husbands and all of her kids died mysteriously and in extraordinary circumstances.

She was living in San Francisco in 1906 when the big quake hit, and the then-20-year-old's husband and their four children died when fire raced through the town. Her husband, Theobold, a cosmetics CEO, had had part of a wall collapse on his leg while her children were trapped upstairs in their home, and Milla claimed she was going to get them help, but no one was ever sure that she did. All we really know is that everyone died in the house, and Milla was seen later that day drinking and dancing in one of the few saloons to survive the destruction.

Six years later, she re-emerged on the first-class deck of *Titanic* with a wealthy English husband, who had made his money in furs, and four new children in tow. Milla often talked about her old life in San Francisco to the other first-class passengers and how she sometimes felt she was cursed. And despite her initial, stated "misgivings" about the *Titanic*, she sailed with her family to New York to attend, with her husband, a New York conference of furriers. She was planning to sample all of the new animal skins there (marmots were red hot that year) and to engage in fur-suit-wearing ribaldry at the event.

Even though the quartermaster Robert Hichens, who was steering the *Titanic* at the fateful moment, survived the sinking, as he was later put in charge of one of the lifeboats, he never spoke on what was rumored to have happened just before the critical ice strike. Scandalous hearsay emerged that Milla Franks had been seen near the wheelhouse when the "Iceberg, right ahead" call had been given and may have disrupted the quartermaster from steering the boat away from the iceberg in those crucial first few moments, though he never testified to that fact at the later inquiry.

What we do know is that after contact, none of Milla Franks' kids or her husband, Bertram, were ever seen on deck afterward, and that Milla danced about for a while before calmly getting into one of the boats alone, with a small collection of her favorite furs, and claimed to have been separated from her family in all the confusion. And she ended up being the family's only survivor.

But that's not the end of the story. Twenty-six years later, Milla Franks' name emerged again in connection with the *Hindenburg*, which she survived, but which claimed her third husband, a jeweler, and the four kids she had produced with him.

The coincidences had piled up, and it really doesn't look too good for Milla Franks, who easily outlived all three of her husbands and her 12 children. When she finally did die, in 1958, at the advanced age of 72, nearly blind, her legs rickety and not anymore reminiscent of the brilliant dancer she once was, she was found in bed, as if she had simply gone to sleep, wrapped in furs, jewels, and with a delicate dusting of rouge on her face, a "Black Widow" whose venom may simply have run out.

---

(27) Eva Silvewicz was a French painter whose work was heavily influenced by the art movements of the era — particularly Expressionism, with its exaggeration of the emotional aspects of life — and Cubism. Her painting *Cubes with Haunted Eyes* meshed the two movements into one unified whole, and her *Emotionally Stunted Cube* set of drawings was likewise unforgettable.

Silvewicz was living in Paris in 1912 and was invited to do a showing of her work at the famed Ashton Masewell Gallery in Greenwich Village. It was the same gallery whose showings had led to artistic breakthroughs for the Artist Dressed as a Cat and also Preston the Real Donkey. But the gallery was looking to break away from its gimmicky animal-based art and saw Silvewicz as a legitimate way to accomplish that. So the company paid her first-class fare to America and promised her all the *ennui* (she was French, after all) she could carry.

Silvewicz boarded the *Titanic* in Cherbourg, after a short *fiacre* (horse-drawn carriage) ride from Paris, the paintings to be displayed wrapped up and along for the voyage with her. The paintings were then accepted and checked in by Roderick Evans, the keeper of the cargo hold. She personally advised the placement of the paintings while the fastidious Evans patiently put up with the instruction, for he certainly knew how to properly pack a cargo hold.

Up on deck most days, painting in the sunshine, Silvewicz enjoyed the rhythms and life aboard the gleaming ship. It was a definite break from her painting studio, where she spent most of her time in solitary work, surrounded by half-finished paintings, spilled paints, spattered smocks, and partially-eaten croissants. The deck bustled with excitement, although most people left her alone with her thoughts, until occasionally a loud-mouthed American, pounding a cigarette noisily onto a cigarette case, would saunter up and demand to know what she was painting.

When the ship hit the iceberg, Silvewicz was asleep, and yet somehow woke up out of an opium stupor to rush for the hold. Roderick Evans assured her the paintings were still undamaged and encouraged her to go upstairs for a nightcap, which Silvewicz did. The nightcap combined with her opium use knocked her out completely, and when she awoke, she was in a lifeboat being lowered into the water. Someone must have spotted her and carried her, unconscious, to her salvation.

Once on the open water, looking up at the ship, she began crying for "my babies," which the startled ship's officer who was rowing eventually came to understand were her paintings. Her "babies" would drown in the cargo hold that night with the man assigned there to their keeping. But, meanwhile, the screams Silvewicz heard coming from the ship over the next two hours, she imagined, were the sounds of agony coming from her art.

After her rescue on the *Carpathia* and delivery to New York City, she shut herself up in a friend's *atelier* and spent the next five years working on a set of paintings that grew out of Expressionism, plus a painting movement she called Titanicism. Her "babies" crying sorrowfully from onboard the *Titanic* became a huge sensation in the Western art world, and Silvewicz lived out her days on a houseboat in eastern Connecticut doing renditions of her "doomed paintings" from the disaster that continued to sell well into her nineties.

10

The Titanic *was full of strivers and dreamers, but it also housed those whose death may not have been the greatest loss to the world.*

(28) Francis Weathers was a NYC slumlord. Enough said?

Weathers was born into a rich family that could be found hitting each other with expensive umbrellas pretty regularly, except on Sundays, when they would walk past a local church and target its congregants for the umbrella abuse. His father, Jeter, began empire building by purchasing properties that had been condemned after a partial collapse and then doing the minimum to improve them, renting them out to poor immigrants as housing that was referred to as "crumble chic."

Francis picked up right where his father left off, hanging an umbrella through one of his belt loops and eventually taking control of a housing empire that was several thousand units strong, only half of which even had running water. He lived on a hill that several of his apartment buildings were at the foot of, and if the residents complained, he would simply walk down to the base of the hill and thrash them with the umbrella. Most of the apartment buildings also had no manager, so getting anything fixed was a labyrinth that often led to a blank wall (and still more umbrella abuse).

Francis had a first-class luxury stateroom on the *Titanic* that was grandly appointed, and he fully expected Hamburg steaks and cola to be delivered at all hours. He often walked the ship, checking the rivets and making sure the ship was reliably put together although he knew it was not how he would have done things. He had a special umbrella stand put together on the ship inside his front door that held up to eight umbrellas, and it was fully stocked and ready.

Examples of problems on board the ship that drew his wrath included but were not limited to: Hamburg steaks that were less-than-adequately warm; Hamburg steaks that were not perfectly symmetrical; Hamburg steaks whose serving plate was visually inadequate; Hamburg steaks that were a tiny bit smaller than usual; and just because.

Weathers was spotted on the fateful night by an escaping family, hitting a ship's officer with an umbrella repeatedly in a hallway while screaming at him, until the officer finally cold-cocked him, leaving him there in a heap in the hallway, where he presumably is to this day.

And as the news of his death spread throughout New York City, a cheerful party atmosphere lit up the day and continued throughout the night in the neighborhoods where his tenements were, and the joy and sustained frivolity led to the collapse of the tallest tenement in that neighborhood. And it was a shame, because if Weathers had been alive, he could have boasted of now having the tallest tenement in the neighborhood.

---

(29) Bailey Benton began stealing before he could walk, which led to some awkwardly slow getaways. When he opened his mouth so the "dirigible" (in those days) could fly in with food on it, there was no telling how often the airship would get hijacked by young Bailey, although his Mom eventually did find a stash of several dozen spoons, years later, beneath a loose floorboard.

And Bailey was no Robin Hood. On the mighty vessel, *Titanic*, rich and poor alike were targets for his silky theft. He might decide to commit a fake fall into the bosom of a socialite, removing a jewel in the process, just as easily as he might make a quick sweep through the third-class cabins, stealing their cheap linens and glass jars. He enjoyed theft for the challenge of theft, and the jewels would be sold later in New York, but most of the third-class property would be cast over the side of the ship at the first opportunity.

Bailey Benton, mid-silky theft.

Bailey had to be more cautious on the voyage than usual because a ship was a self-contained environment where he would be interacting with the same people for five to six days. It would not do to be caught early on, have additional crimes uncovered along the way, and then be reprimanded by a whole steamship full of angry people as he sat in the single padded room on the ship that was used as a holding cell.

One rich and gullible survivor named Clara spoke later about how a man resembling Bailey told her he was a "Canadian Prince" from Alberta, and he had lost his family's jewels, and she felt sorry for him, and gave him a small starter jewel to assuage himself till he could start to rebuild the family fortune. She also told a newspaper that rich people were "skinflints" but also often gave each other jewels if there was a threat another could lose their fortune. "Life was difficult enough," she claimed, "without our exclusive club losing another member to the poors."

There was a report that Bailey may have used the very same jewel he received from Clara to bribe his way onto a lifeboat, although when he hurriedly jumped into the boat, pushing a young girl aside, he slipped on one of the boat's oars and knocked himself out. His head wound worsened overnight on the lifeboat, and he died during the cold evening, as the *Carpathia* steamed toward him, uttering his final words before passing out of the world for good: "Taking all of your spoons, Mummy. You, too, have not immunity from my petty larceny."

---

(30) Lady Eloise Framboise de Burgh was a British countess the crew had been forewarned about a full week before the first boarding when The White Star Line had received a message regarding her from the British government. She was known to be ruthlessly demanding and, when she arrived onboard, even insisted on a private stateroom for her Pekingese dog, Primrose Pharaoh. After nearly every authority onboard informed her that it would be quite impossible to give the dog its own room, she flew into a rage and lit a towering pile of towels on fire.

Lady Eloise also insisted on bringing all her jewelry on board the ship, which she kept in a steamer trunk, and a young Pacific Islander boy wheeled it around quietly behind her. That way she could make jewel changes at any time of day on the fly. The boy was also handcuffed to the steamer trunk, and a burly guard accompanied the group to make sure the boy didn't steal any jewels, because, as Lady Eloise termed it, "You know how those Pacific Islander boys are."

Her dramatics often veered toward dramatic martyrdom. On day four, when she loudly announced a refusal to talk or eat until docked in New York, because her dinner salad had been too cold, it was quite a relief for the crew. And, luckily for them, she held to that vow for most of that day.

She was awakened near midnight on the fateful evening by her jewelry bodyguard right after the boat had struck ice and was hastily ushered to one of the first lifeboats. She broke her vow of silence to demand that Primrose Pharaoh be placed in his very own lifeboat with no other passengers.

Her request was denied, of course, and so, in typical high, dramatic dudgeon, she stood up in the rescue boat in her life jacket with her dog and declared that she would fling herself over the edge into the icy waters if her demands were not met. She then made a move toward the side of the boat, stepped on the hem of her own dress, and accidentally fell in, her beloved Primrose Pharaoh still in her arms. And no one, it's believed, made a move to locate her after the fall. Everyone nearby, as if in a kind of universal understanding, quietly went on their way and silently pretended not to hear the splashes and cries below.

And when the *Mackay-Bennett* bravely picked up over 300 dead bodies floating on the ocean, days later, Lady Eloise Framboise De Burgh was among them, still clinging to her dog, dead eyes staring hard into the cold distance, as if she wished to light a pile of towels on fire in that freezing wasteland and burn the whole thing down.

ACKNOWLEDGMENTS

Thank you to everyone who has helped me along the way to my first novel. You know who you are.

Okay, okay, relax, I'll tell people who you are.

Profound thanks, first off, goes to Brian Boone, editor extraordinaire, whose superb advice and upbeat nature kept me ebulliently believing that this was a very worthwhile endeavor. Also, to Marty Dundics, for the artwork and for giving me the opportunity in the first place.

Also of tremendous value, the wise counsel of Mike Hughes and John O'Malley.

And at different stages of the words, oversized kudos are presented to Matt Manser, Brian Kiley, Tamra Brown, Martha Kelly, Raj Desai, Jessie Gaskell, Mark Ganek, Gregory Martin, and Bennie Arthur. And thanks to some of my inspiration gurus, Jen Spyra, Alicia Bien, Brian O'Connell, Emo Philips, Robin Groves, and Erick Feigin. And to my writing partners in other realms (plus their long-term friendship), Gil Rief and Kimberly Clark, I can't say enough.

Also, a special shoutout to the people like Doug Karo, Tom

Repetto, and Anthony Jeselnik who helped point my way into the entertainment business.

Also, thanks to my mom, dad, and sister, and my family scattered around New Hampshire, Virginia, and Massachusetts. We have a fairly small but joyful family that laughs a lot, and it makes it feel like the biggest and funnest party when we're all together. Also, the best to a long list of funny and inspirational standup, sketch, and short film friends over the years, a large percentage of whom were hanging out at one time or another at The UCB, The Improv, and especially the IO in Los Angeles, before it closed and became a drug and weapons den.

Finally, to my wife, Yuki (AGAIN! -- see dedication), for your love and constant encouragement. And to her family. I was welcomed into the family quite a while ago, and they have been nothing but nice to me. Thank you.

ABOUT THE AUTHOR

Shawn Carlow is a writer and producer who has worked for *Late Night with Jimmy Fallon*, *Jimmy Kimmel Live!*, and *Deon Cole's Black Box*, among others. He's written jokes for stage, radio, and various standup comics.

In addition, he does stand-up comedy himself and has made a number of award-winning comic short films that were shown at various live shows and on CBS. He has a wife and a cat.

People of the Titanic is his first work of fiction.

www.ingramcontent.com/pod-product-compliance
Lightning Source LLC
Chambersburg PA
CBHW071950190726
48293CB00004B/1419

* 9 7 8 1 9 5 4 1 5 8 3 6 8 *